NATIONAL GEOGRAPHIC

YANKEE BLUE
—OR—
REBEL GRAY?

THE CIVIL WAR ADVENTURES OF SAM SHAW

KATE CONNELL

PICTURE CREDITS
Cover from the original painting by Mort Künstler, "High Water Mark" ©
1988 Mort Künstler, Inc.; cover (inset) and p. 6 (bot. le.) courtesy Paul
Robert Jordan; pp. 1, 28-29 Engraving after F.O.C. Darley, Tinted by P.
Hall Baglie; pp. 2–3, 4 (inset), 6 (except bot. le.), 7, 8–9, 12 (inset),
14–15, 16–17, 18 (inset), 19 (inset), 20–21, 22 (inset), 24–25, 26–27,
30–31, 32–33, 36–37 Library of Congress; p. 4–5 Gerald A. Massie;
pp. 10–11, 12–13, Frank and Marie-Therese Wood Print Collections,
Alexandria, VA; p. 18–19 The State Museum of Pennsylvania,
Pennsylvania Historical and Museum Commission; p. 22–23 Richard
Schlecht; p. 34–35 Tom Lovell/NG Image Collection; p. 38–39 Thad
Samuels Abell II/NG Image Collection.

Library of Congress Cataloging-in-Publication Data
Connell, Kate, 1954-
    Yankee blue or Rebel gray: the Civil War adventures of Sam Shaw / by
Kate Connell.
        p. cm. — (I am American)
    Summary: Illustrated text, letters, and diary excerpts follow the fic-
tional Abbotts in Ohio, whose son fights for the Union, and their rela-
tives in Tennessee, who support the Confederacy, during the Civil War.
    ISBN 0-7922-5179-2 (pbk.)
    1. United States—History—Civil War, 1861–1865—Social aspects—
Juvenile lieterature. 2. Soldiers—United States—History—19th cen-
tury—Juvenile literature. 3. Soldiers—Confederate States of
America—History—Juvenile literature. 4. United States—History—
Civil War, 1861–1865—Campaigns—Juvenile literature. [1. United
States—History—Civil War, 1861–1865. 2. Soldiers. 3. Confederate
States of America.] I. Title. II. Series.

E468.9C66 2002
973.7'1—dc21
                                2002044926

Produced through the worldwide resources of the National Geographic
Society, John M. Fahey, Jr., President and Chief Executive Officer;
Gilbert M. Grosvenor, Chairman of the Board; Nina D. Hoffman,
Executive Vice President and President, Books and Education
Publishing; Ericka Markman, President, Children's Books and Education
Publishing Group; Steve Mico, Vice President Education Publishing
Group, Editorial Director; Marianne Hiland, Editorial Manager; Anita
Schwartz, Project Editor; Tara Peterson, Editorial Assistant; Jim Hiscott,
Design Manager; Linda McKnight, Art Director; Diana Bourdrez, Anne
Whittle, Photo Research; Matt Wascavage, Manager of Publishing
Services; Sean Philpotts, Production Coordinator.

Production: Clifton M. Brown III, Manufacturing and Quality Control

PROGRAM DEVELOPMENT: Gare Thompson Associates, Inc.

BOOK DESIGN: Herman Adler Design

Published by the National Geographic Society
1145 17th Street, N.W.
Washington, D.C. 20036-4688

Printed in Spain

TABLE of CONTENTS

A HOUSE DIVIDING

The Civil War was a war of Americans against Americans. It was fought on American soil. Neighbors fought against neighbors. Cousins fought against cousins. Even brothers fought against each other.

At the root of the struggle was the issue of slavery. In 1860 Americans elected a new president, Abraham Lincoln. Lincoln had promised not to end slavery in the states where it already existed. Most people in the South did not believe him. After his election, South Carolina **seceded** from, or left, the **Union**. (The Union was another name for the United States.) Six other states followed in January 1861. Together the states formed their own nation, the Confederate States of America.

Oregon

California

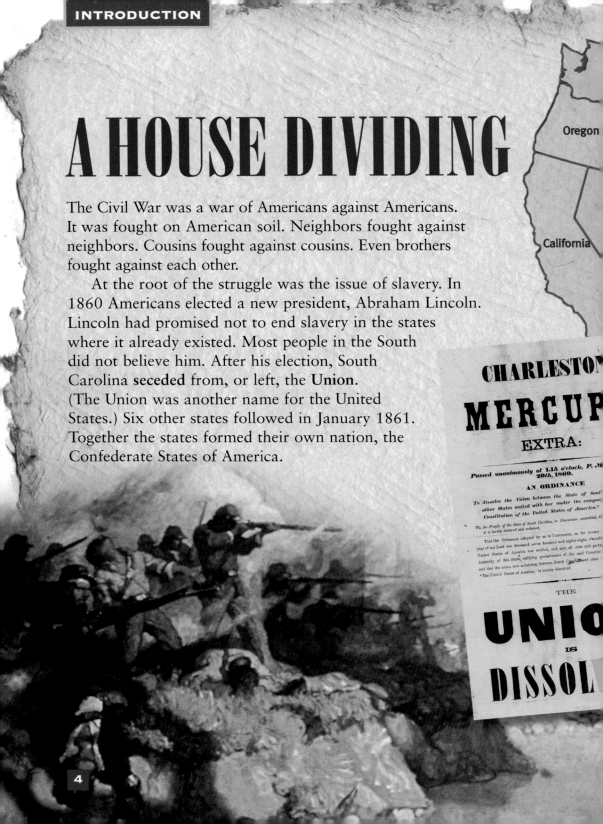

CHARLESTON

MERCUR

EXTRA:

Passed unanimously at 1.15 o'clock, P. M
20th, 1860.

AN ORDINANCE

To dissolve the Union between the State of Sout
other States united with her under the compac
Constitution of the United States of America."

THE

UNIO

IS

DISSOL

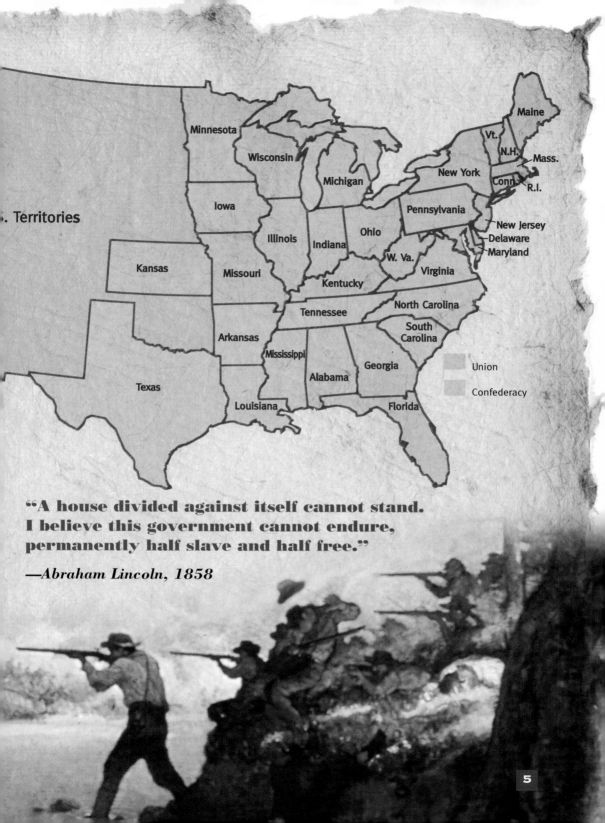

Territories

Minnesota

Wisconsin

Michigan

Maine

Vt.

N.H.

Mass.

New York

Conn.

R.I.

Iowa

Pennsylvania

New Jersey

Delaware

Maryland

Illinois

Indiana

Ohio

W. Va.

Kansas

Missouri

Kentucky

Virginia

Tennessee

North Carolina

Arkansas

South Carolina

Mississippi

Georgia

Alabama

Union

Confederacy

Texas

Louisiana

Florida

"A house divided against itself cannot stand. I believe this government cannot endure, permanently half slave and half free."

—*Abraham Lincoln, 1858*

THE SHAW FAMILY

THE ABBOTT FAMILY

Samuel Shaw,
father

Julia Shaw,
mother

Edwina Abbott,
mother

Dr. Thomas Abbott,
father

Eli, 20

Marietta, 17

Henry, 19

Sam, 13

CHAPTER 1

CHOOSING SIDES

It was March, 1861. Texas joined the **Confederacy.** Now seven states in the South had left the Union. The other slaveholding states had decided not to secede—yet.

Tennessee was one southern state that had voted to stay in the Union. Uncertainty was in the air. What would President Lincoln do? Would he let the South go without a fight? If war broke out, what would Tennessee do?

People everywhere wrestled with the question, *Which side am I on?* That choice sometimes split families apart. This is what happened to the Shaws and the Abbotts, cousins from Tennessee and Ohio.

In Columbus, Ohio, Dr. Thomas Abbott and his wife, Edwina, were loyal Unionists. They believed the Union should remain united. Hundreds of miles to the south, on a farm near Franklin, Tennessee, Edwina's sister, Julia Shaw, lived with her family. The Shaws supported the Confederacy.

On April 12, 1861, Confederate forces attacked Fort Sumter in Charleston, South Carolina. This fort belonged to the national government. War had begun. This is the story of the Abbotts and the Shaws during the Civil War. It is told through their diaries and letters.

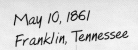

May 10, 1861
Franklin, Tennessee

Dear Edwina,

I have much to tell you. How life here has changed in the past few days.

Have you seen the newspapers? Since the attack on Fort Sumter, President Lincoln has called for volunteers. He is raising a large army. This news electrified the young men in our area. All rushed to join the Confederate Army. They all swear to do or die for the Confederacy.

As a result, the event which I have been dreading happened. Eli rode to Nashville yesterday morning to join up. He will be a private in the First Tennessee Infantry. He is as excited as a small boy, no matter that he is a man of twenty. Young Sam looks at him as if he were a god.

But I, dear sister, feel only great sorrow mixed with pride. How I fear what war may do to him! But our cause is just. We fight for our right to live as we choose. If the government will send an army to trample upon this right, then we must rise and defend our honor.

Your affectionate sister,
Julia

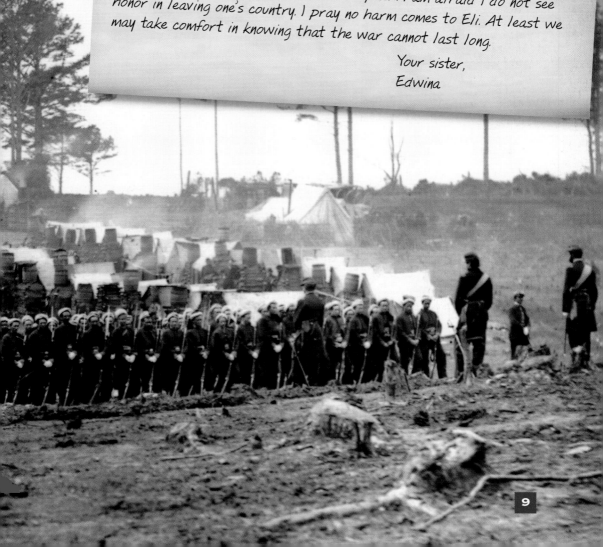

May 25, 1861
Columbus, Ohio

Dear Julia,

    Here in Ohio "war fever" is raging. The people are wild for the Union. Henry, too, is thinking of enlisting! I have begged him to wait awhile.

    President Lincoln asked for thirteen regiments of soldiers from this state. But so many young men have enlisted that he must take twenty. Flags fly everywhere. Even little girls show their patriotism with red, white, and blue ribbons in their bonnets.

    You and I both know that Lincoln's call to arms will push Tennessee to secede. You say this is the honorable path. I am afraid I do not see honor in leaving one's country. I pray no harm comes to Eli. At least we may take comfort in knowing that the war cannot last long.

Your sister,
Edwina

9

From Sam's journal

June 15, 1861

Eli gave me this book to write down what happens while he's away fighting the Yankees. He'll read it when the war's over. That should be by Christmas, he says.

Pa says Tennessee voted to leave the Union. Hurrah! Now we'll have our own country. No more Yankees telling us what to do. We got a letter from Aunt Edwina. She says Henry wants to join up with the Yankees, but he hasn't yet. I sure hope Eli and Henry don't have to shoot at each other.

July 10, 1861

Eli's company left for Virginia. We rode to Nashville to see them off. They looked right smart in their uniforms. Ma made Eli's. The send-off was like a carnival. There was a parade and speeches and ladies dressed up. Pa says Virginia's where the fighting's going to be. I wish I could go.

August 2, 1861

Eli wrote. Bad news. He missed the first big battle of the war! It was at a place in Virginia called Manassas Junction. The Rebels whipped the Yankees! They sent them running back to Washington to hide behind old Lincoln's hat. Eli's company got there after the fighting ended. I hope the war lasts a little longer so Eli gets another chance.

September 5, 1861
Columbus, Ohio

Dear Sister,

Henry has enlisted! I believe I wrote telling you that he wanted to enlist. He held back for my sake. In July, Henry became friendly with Cass Sherman, a young man here. Cass is a student at Oberlin College. Oberlin is a very unusual school, as it admits both women and Negroes. Cass invited Henry to visit the college and visit Cleveland. Thomas and I let him go.

But Oberlin was the wrong place for my boy. The people there are passionately in support of the Union. When word came of the Union defeat at Bull Run (which you call Manassas), Henry caught their passion. He and Cass enlisted together at Camp Wood, near Cleveland. He will be a private in the 41st Ohio Infantry.

Henry is now training at Camp Wood. Thomas and I will see him next week. In the meantime, I keep busy sewing his uniform. When I think about his leaving, the tears come.

Though I expected this, it still comes as a blow! May God help me to bear it.

Always your affectionate,
Edwina

Edwina Abbott and Julia Shaw were like thousands of mothers, wives, and sisters of Civil War soldiers. They grieved when their loved ones went to war. Then they dried their tears and went on with their lives.

Such women helped the war effort in many ways. They ran farms and businesses while their men were away. They sewed uniforms and made bandages at home. Thousands served as nurses. Others set up aid societies. Still others worked as spies, in weapons factories, or in government offices. Hundreds of brave women even dressed as men and became soldiers.

With so many soldiers and their families separated, the amount of mail increased greatly during the war years. In the early months of the war, one Union **regiment** of 1,000 men sent out 600 letters a day! Mail call was the high point of a soldier's day. Letters from home were greeted with shouts—sometimes tears—of joy.

CHAPTER 2

LIVING with the ENEMY

After several weeks of military training, Henry Abbott's regiment was sent to Kentucky. It stayed there, waiting for orders, through the winter.

Then, in February of 1862, the Union Army won its first great victory. An unknown Union commander, Ulysses S. Grant, captured two key forts in Tennessee—Fort Henry and Fort Donelson. These forts had been built to protect Nashville and middle Tennessee against a Union invasion.

The order came for Union troops to advance on Nashville. The people in the city fled. The Confederate Army destroyed arms, supplies, and factories so the Union troops couldn't use them. They burned bridges to slow the Union Army down.

On February 25, Union troops entered Nashville. The mayor surrendered the city. More Union troops continued to arrive. Among them was the 41st Ohio, Henry Abbott's regiment.

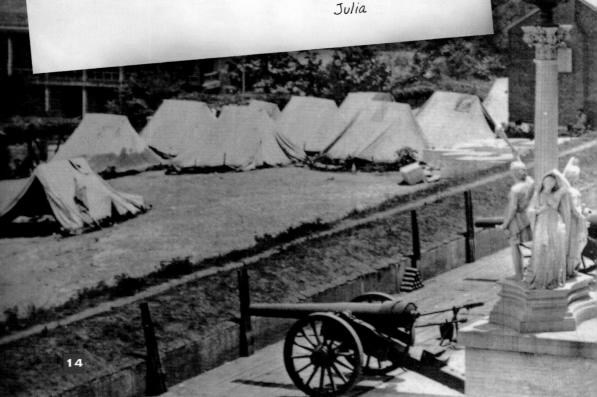

March 1, 1862
Franklin, Tennessee

Dear Edwina,

I hardly know where to begin. What I have to tell will please you, I hope. You must know by now that Nashville has fallen. For days, the unhappy citizens streamed out of the city. Carts and wagons filled the roads going south. Many fleeing people asked for food as they passed our farm. We gave what we could.

Others did not ask but simply stole. Samuel took to sitting up nights with a shotgun across his lap.

Then yesterday two Union soldiers rode into our yard. I trembled inside but went to meet them with a calm face. Imagine my relief and joy when I recognized dear, dear Henry! With him was his friend Cass Sherman.

Henry and Cass were in high spirits and made us all laugh. Only young Sam was sulky. He thinks anyone in a blue uniform is a devil. But it was a fine visit. For a short while we were able to forget the war. I will write more of Henry when I can. He sends his love.

Your sister,
Julia

From Sam's journal

March 3, 1862
Henry came here two days ago. I don't understand how he could fight against the South, after all the time he has spent in Tennessee. But he's kin so I didn't say anything. Cass is here again, visiting Marietta. Whatever he says, she laughs and flutters her eyes at him. I might just be sick.

March 10, 1862
Franklin, Tennessee

Dear Edwina,

This letter will be short and gloomy. The mood in the countryside is ugly. Now that the Union troops hold Nashville, their soldiers are living in all the surrounding towns. In this way they hope to control the countryside.

I had hoped that Henry would stay in Franklin, so he could be close by. Now I am glad he is not. There is talk that the local men plan to attack the Union soldiers at night. Young Sam wants to help. We are keeping a close eye on him, especially at night.

Marietta is another worry. Cass Sherman visits her too often. If we were not at war, I would be pleased, for Cass is a good boy. But he is also the "enemy." (So is Henry, though it breaks my heart to say it.) There is so much hatred of the Yankees. I fear for our safety but especially for Marietta's.

Your sister,
Julia

From Sam's journal

March 19, 1862

Heard Pa say some Union men were shot at last night. Go, Rebels! I wonder how I can help them. Union troops left Nashville yesterday, including Henry's regiment. They headed south. I hope they meet up with some of our soldiers down there. They'll give those Ohio boys a licking. (Except for Henry, that is.) I'm right glad they're gone. I thought Ma would be unhappy, but she seems relieved.

April 5, 1862
Franklin, Tennessee

Dear Edwina,

This war will be our ruin. As yet, we have not suffered greatly. But I see where we are heading.

Young Sam is longing to strike a blow against the Yankees. The father of one of his friends is a bushwhacker who hides in the woods and attacks the Yankees without any warning. This man and his kind are daily becoming bolder. I fear that Sam will follow their example.

Marietta makes no effort to hide her feelings for Cass. Foolish girl! Her friends treat her coldly. But the real danger lies with the bushwhackers. They will harm anyone who seems to be for the Union, even a lovestruck girl. We are all in danger.

The crops are coming in nicely. I expect the Union soldiers will take most of what we harvest. When I feel angry, I think of Henry and Cass. I hope that some Confederate farm woman will swallow her anger and feed them when they are hungry.

No letter from Eli in two weeks.

Your sister,
Julia

Union supply wagons crossing a bridge

After Nashville surrendered, President Lincoln put middle Tennessee under military rule. He sent Andrew Johnson, a native of Tennessee and a loyal Unionist, to serve as military governor. The towns around Nashville were **occupied**, or controlled, by Union soldiers.

The townsfolk were open in their hatred of the Yankees. They called them names, spat at them, and refused to associate with them. But the Union presence was too strong for them to do more.

In the countryside, where the Shaws lived, things were different. The Unionists couldn't patrol every road and village. Bushwhackers attacked Union patrols. They stole or destroyed Union property. They attacked anyone who showed loyalty to the Union.

The occupation was to last for the rest of the war. In that time, hundreds of incidents—**raids**, killings, house burnings—would take place. Julia Shaw was right. Things were going to get worse.

CHAPTER 3

SHILOH

Ulysses S. Grant

Henry Abbott's Ohio regiment marched out of Nashville in March. They were headed for Savannah, Tennessee, to join General Grant's army. They got there on Saturday, April 5.

General Grant was waiting at Pittsburg Landing on the Tennessee River. He planned to invade Mississippi. What Grant didn't know was that a large Confederate Army had marched north to meet him. Eli Shaw's regiment was part of this army.

On the morning of April 6, the Rebels opened fire and charged into the Union camp. For two days the fighting raged. It was the first taste of battle for Eli Shaw and Henry Abbott.

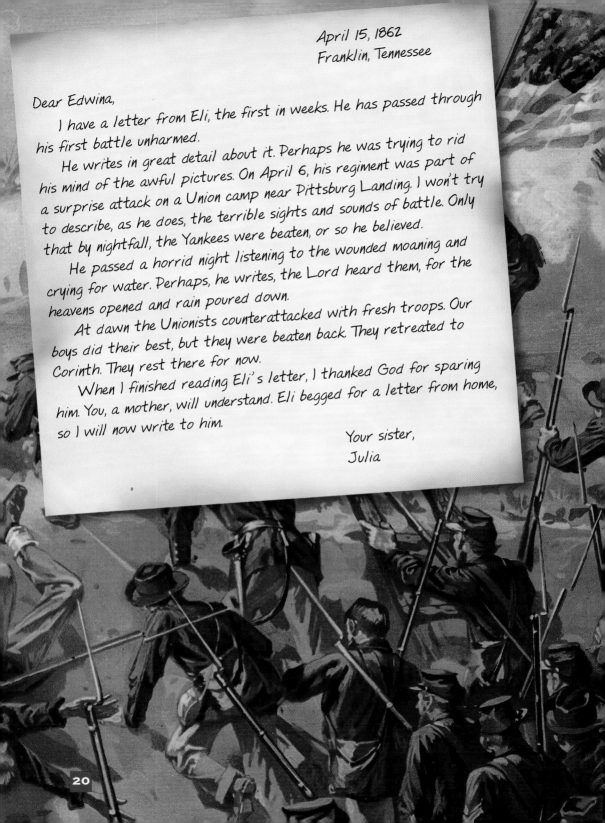

April 15, 1862
Franklin, Tennessee

Dear Edwina,

I have a letter from Eli, the first in weeks. He has passed through his first battle unharmed.

He writes in great detail about it. Perhaps he was trying to rid his mind of the awful pictures. On April 6, his regiment was part of a surprise attack on a Union camp near Pittsburg Landing. I won't try to describe, as he does, the terrible sights and sounds of battle. Only that by nightfall, the Yankees were beaten, or so he believed.

He passed a horrid night listening to the wounded moaning and crying for water. Perhaps, he writes, the Lord heard them, for the heavens opened and rain poured down.

At dawn the Unionists counterattacked with fresh troops. Our boys did their best, but they were beaten back. They retreated to Corinth. They rest there for now.

When I finished reading Eli's letter, I thanked God for sparing him. You, a mother, will understand. Eli begged for a letter from home, so I will now write to him.

Your sister,
Julia

April 28, 1862
Columbus, Ohio

Dear Julia,

My news is bad, too. I have a letter from Henry. His regiment was among the Union troops that beat back your Rebels at Pittsburg Landing. I cannot bear the thought of our two boys on the same battlefield, shooting at each other. And yet the thought won't go away.

I rejoice that Henry came through his first fight without injury. But with great sadness, I must tell you that Cass Sherman was killed. Henry writes that he fought bravely until a single bullet struck his forehead. He died at once and did not suffer.

We were both fond of the boy. But Marietta will feel it most. Tell her as you see fit, or wait to hear from Henry. He is writing to her.

Your sister,
Edwina

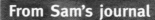

From Sam's journal

May 15, 1862

Cass Sherman is dead. He took a Rebel bullet in the same battle Eli was in. Pa says both sides took a bad licking, but the Yankees won.

I wonder if Eli shot Cass. If he could've shot Cass, he could've shot Henry just as well. That ain't right. I feel bad for Marietta. Didn't like Cass, but it still ain't right.

I don't like this war like I used to.

The battle near Pittsburg Landing came to be called Shiloh. Its name came from a log church, Shiloh Church, which means "church of peace." Some of the fiercest fighting went on there.

Most of the soldiers who fought at Shiloh were untested. Like Henry Abbott and Eli Shaw, they had never been in battle before. As a result, discipline was poor. Many **deserted** and ran away. Some mistakenly shot at their own troops. Out of 100,000 men who fought, over 20,000 were killed, wounded, captured, or missing.

Before Shiloh, many in the South boasted that one Southerner was as good as several Northerners in a fight. Shiloh taught them that this wasn't true.

The North learned something, too. Until Shiloh, many Northerners thought the South would soon give up. After Shiloh, they realized that they would have to defeat the South to stop the war.

CHAPTER 4

HOME, SWEET HOME

Americans were horrified by Shiloh. Yet such terrible bloodshed became normal in this cruel war. Five months after Shiloh, there were about 23,000 **casualties** in one day at Antietam. Losses were no longer counted in hundreds, or even thousands, but in tens of thousands: 29,600 at Chancellorsville; over 51,000 at Gettysburg; 34,700 at Chickamauga.

By Christmas of 1863, Henry Abbott and Eli Shaw had both seen plenty of fighting. After a loss at Chattanooga, the First Tennessee Infantry **retreated** to winter quarters in Georgia. They were hungry, tattered, and worn out.

The 41st Ohio were the victors, but they were exhausted. They were given **furloughs** and allowed to go home for a short rest. In February, Henry Abbott went home.

Map painting of the Battle of Shiloh

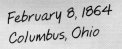

February 8, 1864
Columbus, Ohio

Dear Julia,

 Henry is home! He arrived here on the 4th. It is a joy to have him home. I only wish it were permanent.

 The war is changing Henry. He was promoted again, to second lieutenant. He looks so serious. Last evening we invited a small company of friends and neighbors to meet him. Talk turned to the war, of course. Everyone praised Grant. Many think he will defeat the Rebels.

 Henry described the battle for Chattanooga. He told us of his regiment's final march, barefoot through the snow. Yet this was nothing, he said, compared to what the Rebels suffer. They are continually starving, ragged, and barefoot. They desert by the dozens. We pray for Eli.

 We will have five weeks with our boy. He is wild to see people and have a good time. We have theater tickets for Saturday. I prefer to stay quietly at home together until he must go back But I will do whatever pleases him.

Your affectionate sister,
Edwina

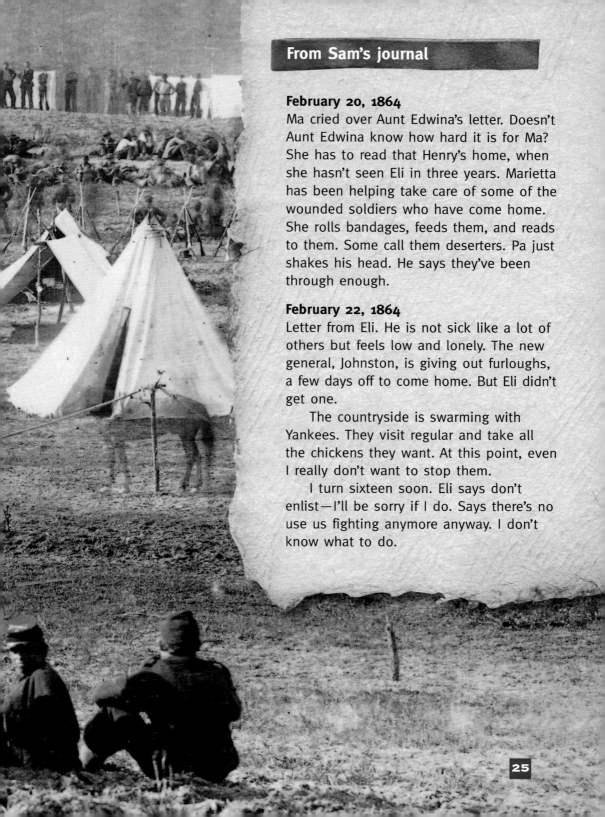

From Sam's journal

February 20, 1864
Ma cried over Aunt Edwina's letter. Doesn't Aunt Edwina know how hard it is for Ma? She has to read that Henry's home, when she hasn't seen Eli in three years. Marietta has been helping take care of some of the wounded soldiers who have come home. She rolls bandages, feeds them, and reads to them. Some call them deserters. Pa just shakes his head. He says they've been through enough.

February 22, 1864
Letter from Eli. He is not sick like a lot of others but feels low and lonely. The new general, Johnston, is giving out furloughs, a few days off to come home. But Eli didn't get one.

The countryside is swarming with Yankees. They visit regular and take all the chickens they want. At this point, even I really don't want to stop them.

I turn sixteen soon. Eli says don't enlist—I'll be sorry if I do. Says there's no use us fighting anymore anyway. I don't know what to do.

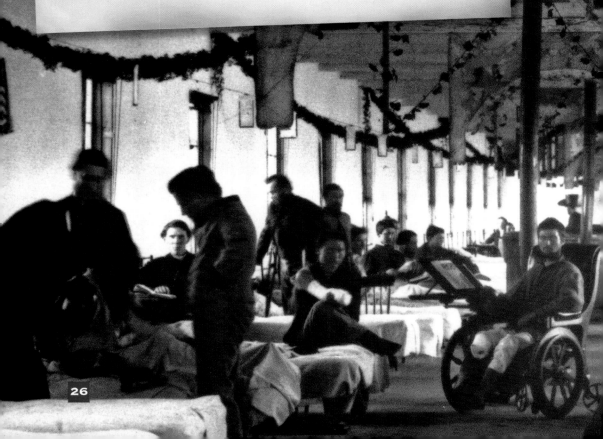

February 24, 1864
Franklin, Tennessee

Dear Edwina,

I am pleased for you that Henry is home. Life continues to be hard here. Eli didn't get a furlough. We must hold on until the end, I suppose, before we see him. I pray he returns to us.

A short while back three Unionists in our county were murdered by a bushwhacker. The Yankee troops knew who the killer was but were unable to find him. A week later, the Yankees killed the man's father and burned down his grandfather's house. They all do the work of the devil, Yankees and bushwackers alike.

Marietta has moved to Nashville. She is boarding with the family you suggested; a very good family indeed. She now works in a Union hospital there that used to be a church. Young Sam is my only child left at home now.

Your sister,
Julia

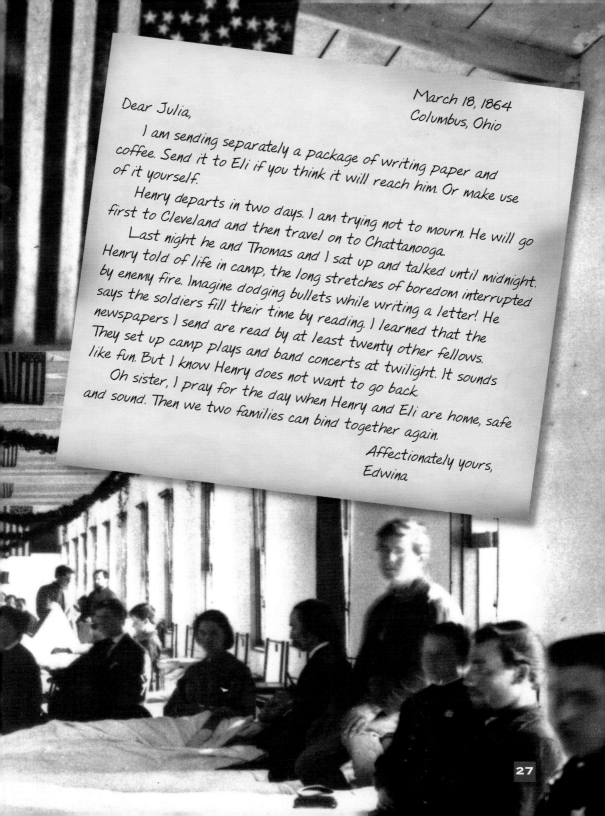

March 18, 1864
Columbus, Ohio

Dear Julia,

I am sending separately a package of writing paper and coffee. Send it to Eli if you think it will reach him. Or make use of it yourself.

Henry departs in two days. I am trying not to mourn. He will go first to Cleveland and then travel on to Chattanooga.

Last night he and Thomas and I sat up and talked until midnight. Henry told of life in camp, the long stretches of boredom interrupted by enemy fire. Imagine dodging bullets while writing a letter! He says the soldiers fill their time by reading. I learned that the newspapers I send are read by at least twenty other fellows. They set up camp plays and band concerts at twilight. It sounds like fun. But I know Henry does not want to go back.

Oh sister, I pray for the day when Henry and Eli are home, safe and sound. Then we two families can bind together again.

Affectionately yours,
Edwina

As the war dragged on, it became ever more important to keep up the soldiers' spirits. One way to do this was to let soldiers visit their families. Henry Abbott returned from his furlough with new energy.

On the other hand, Eli Shaw felt his spirits sink lower and lower. Like most people in the spring of 1864, he realized that the South was losing the war.

In July of 1863, the Union Army had won two key victories. It had beaten the Confederates, led by general Robert E. Lee, at Gettysburg. It had also taken the city of Vicksburg on the Mississippi River.

The Confederate Army was underfed and poorly clothed. Thousands were dying of disease. Soldiers got letters describing terrible hardships at home. Many soldiers went home to join their families, although the punishment for desertion might be death.

CHAPTER 5

The BATTLE of FRANKLIN

In the spring of 1864, the Union Army left Chattanooga. They were under the command of William Tecumseh Sherman. The troops began a slow advance toward the largest city in the deep South, Atlanta, Georgia. The Union troops (including Henry's regiment) forced the Rebels (including Eli's regiment) to retreat.

In September, Atlanta fell. Sherman's army began a destructive march through Georgia to the city of Savannah on the coast.

The morning of November 30, 1864, found the Union troops in a strong position. They were at the southern edge of Franklin—not five miles from the Shaw farm. The Confederate General Hood's shrinking army faced them across two miles of open fields. At about 4:00 P.M., Hood ordered the first of 13 hopeless **charges** against the Union defenses.

November 30, 1864
Franklin, Tennessee

Dearest Sister,

I write by candlelight, not sure if you will receive this letter. We have had many terrible days since this war began. But this day was the worst. Since late this afternoon a battle has been raging just west of our farm.

It is now long past dark. Yet the battle does not end. As I write this, I tremble from the roar of the guns. It fills my ears and shakes the house. The night sky is alive with the glow of exploding shells. Samuel sits with me, his face grim as death. He holds a shotgun.

And young Sam is here. Oh, Edwina, the worst part of this awful day was that Sam ran off without telling us. He went to see the fighting. We were wild with fright. Samuel was about to go look for him when Sam walked in the door. He was dirty and breathless but whole. Samuel scolded him severely. Added to our anxiety is our constant fear that this battle will take Eli from us for good.

I will close now. We have never agreed about this war. But in all else you have been close to my heart.

Affectionately,
Julia

From Sam's journal

December 1, 1864
Watched the fighting yesterday. It was horrible. Hundreds of men, like swarms of ants, moving on the plain. Flashes of gunfire everywhere. A popping, sizzling sound when they fire all at once. Smoke hanging over everything. And the guns— it's enough to deafen a person. I was so scared for Eli.

Pa intends to look for Eli today, to find out if he's living. Or to claim his body if he isn't.

December 2, 1864
Went with Pa, but didn't find Eli. We looked at Carnton plantation, where Rebel wounded fill every room and cover the floor. The smell and the cries of the men! I felt sick to my stomach.

We searched town. Nearly every house and building is a hospital. Spent hours on the battlefield. Can't say for sure that Eli wasn't among the corpses, there were so many.

December 3, 1864
I'm afraid to write this. I went into the barn this morning at dawn and Eli was there, hiding. He looks awful—skinny, dirty, ragged, no shoes, and a look in his eye like a whipped dog. What should I do? I heard they sometimes shoot deserters.

From Sam's journal

December 4, 1864

I told Pa. He went to the barn alone. Came back and sat for a spell without talking. Then he said, "Ma, our boy's home." She turned pale.

We snuck Eli into the house. Ma cried to see him so low and scared. She cooked for him. He ate and ate like an animal. Then we sat together. Finally Pa said, "Boy, you have got to go back." Eli said, "I know." He went after dark. Pa gave him his coat and his shoes. I know Eli had to go back, but I hated to see him go. I wish this war was over. I don't care who wins. I never saw Ma so torn up.

December 31, 1864
Franklin, Tennessee

Dear Edwina,

I wrote you a letter which I never sent. I am sending it now so that you may know what we have gone through. Read it before you read this.

Eli survived the battle at Franklin. But his spirits were crushed. He deserted his regiment and came here. My heart broke at the sight of him. Harder still was watching him go back. Why did I let him go? How could I let him go? I know not how. But it was the right thing to do. Our cause may be lost, but we will never sacrifice our honor.

I learned from the townspeople that the 41st Ohio, Henry's regiment, did not fight at Franklin. They were protecting the bridge which the army passed over as they left town.

Two weeks ago the armies clashed again outside of Nashville. Our boys lost. The Unionists chased them south. They may be chasing them still for all I know. I've heard that Union troops are destroying houses, barns, and buildings along the way. Samuel thinks this is the end of the war in the west. I pray he is right.

Your sister,
Julia

Ruins of a building in Richmond, Virginia, the Confederate capital

Samuel Shaw was right. The battle of Nashville was the end of heavy fighting in the West. It was one of the rare times in the war that a Confederate Army fled the field. Chased by Union forces, they retreated south for ten days. When they crossed the Tennessee River in Alabama, the Unionists let them go.

The survivors of the Confederate Army of Tennessee made their way to Mississippi and Alabama. Those who had not deserted by then (and that included Eli Shaw) were sent east to the Carolinas.

In late March, the shrunken Confederate forces made a desperate attempt to stop Sherman's army in North Carolina. They fought for three days before giving up. It was the last battle of the war for Eli Shaw and the Confederate Army of Tennessee.

CHAPTER 6

The END of the WAR

On April 9, 1865, Robert E. Lee, the commander of the Confederate forces, surrendered his army to Ulysses S. Grant at Appomattox Court House in Virginia. Grant offered Lee generous terms which he accepted with great appreciation. Confederate soldiers were allowed to keep their horses and mules for spring planting and to go home in peace.

When the country heard news of the agreement, bells rang out and bands played. But the celebration was short-lived. On April 15, President Abraham Lincoln was assassinated.

April 11, 1865
Columbus, Ohio

Dear Julia,

The news of the Confederacy's surrender has lifted a great weight from all our hearts. At last this cursed war is over. It is over! (I must wipe my tears.)

Yesterday businesses and schools were closed for a day of celebration. Cannons were fired, songs were sung, speeches were made. Flags again fly everywhere. The city looks much as it did at the beginning of the war. But the feeling is different. Then, we were plunging into a firestorm, not knowing what lay ahead. Now, we have come through the fire and are again one nation. It is hard-won happiness indeed.

The surrender must be a relief to you, Rebel though you are. Write and tell me of Eli. After wintering in Huntsville, Alabama, Henry is in East Tennessee. He writes that he will soon be ordered to Nashville. He will try to see you.

Your affectionate sister,
Edwina

April 15, 1865

Lincoln died this morning, shot by John Booth, a Rebel. Pa heard the news when he rode into town. It came in on the army telegraph. When Pa got back, he walked out to where I was plowing and told me.

While we were at war, I hated Lincoln. But you do not shoot the President while he is watching a play with his wife. That is the work of a coward!

April 20, 1865
Columbus, Ohio

Dear Julia,

How quickly joy turns to sorrow! We are all in mourning for the President.

We learned in the papers that Lincoln's funeral train will be passing through Cleveland. A special shelter is being built in Monument Square where his body will lie. They expect thousands of mourners. Thomas and I will be among them. We will take the rail car to Cleveland early next week.

Your sorrowing sister,
Edwina

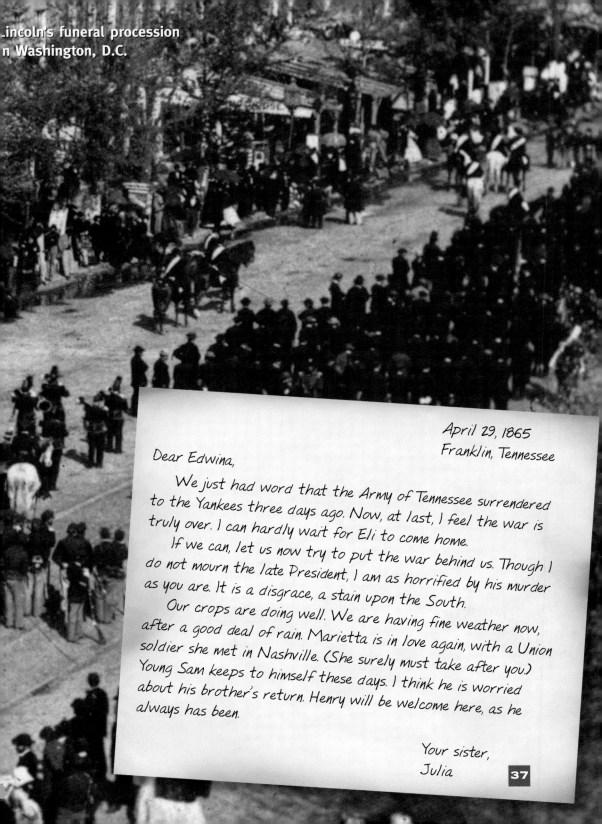

April 29, 1865
Franklin, Tennessee

Dear Edwina,

We just had word that the Army of Tennessee surrendered to the Yankees three days ago. Now, at last, I feel the war is truly over. I can hardly wait for Eli to come home.

If we can, let us now try to put the war behind us. Though I do not mourn the late President, I am as horrified by his murder as you are. It is a disgrace, a stain upon the South.

Our crops are doing well. We are having fine weather now, after a good deal of rain. Marietta is in love again, with a Union soldier she met in Nashville. (She surely must take after you.) Young Sam keeps to himself these days. I think he is worried about his brother's return. Henry will be welcome here, as he always has been.

Your sister,
Julia

37

EPILOGUE

With the war over, the Shaws and the Abbotts faced the same enormous task that faced the entire country: to put the war behind them. It wasn't easy.

By the time Eli came home, Henry was in Nashville with his regiment. When Henry visited the Shaws, the two cousins came face to face. One was a victorious Union officer. The other was a defeated yet fiercely proud Rebel. On the surface, the visit was cordial. But underneath, feelings of pride, sorrow, and bitterness ran strong.

Henry returned to live with his parents in Ohio. After two years of trying different jobs, Henry rejoined the army. He was sent out west as a career officer. He married a Native American woman and remained in the West.

It took Eli many months to recover from his wartime experiences. He worked on the farm and eventually married. When his father died, he took over the farm. Marietta married her Union soldier and moved to Detroit, Michigan. Young Sam surprised everyone. He went to college in Nashville and became a professor of American history.

Julia and Edwina wrote to each other for the rest of their lives. But they never completely regained the closeness they had before war divided them.

Cemetery at Fort Donelson, Tennessee

GLOSSARY

casualties – people injured or killed in a war

Confederacy – the Confederate States of America

charge – an attack

desert – to run away from the army

furlough – time off from duty for military people

occupied – captured and controlled

raid – a sudden attack

regiment – a unit of troops made up of two or more battalions

retreat – to move back

secede – to withdraw from a group or an organization

Union – the United States of America